Fearless Freddie

by Shelley Swanson Sateren

illustrated by Deborah Melmon

CONTENTS

ADVENTURES
—AT—
HOUND HOTEL

IT'S TIME FOR YOUR ADVENTURE AT HOUND HOTEL!

At Hound Hotel, dogs are given the royal treatment. We are a top-notch boarding kennel. When your dog stays with us, we will follow your feeding schedule, take them for walks and tuck them into bed at night.

We are just a short walk away from the dogs — the kennels are located in a heated building at the end of our driveway. Every dog has his or her own kennel, with a bed, blanket and water bowl.

Rest assured ... a stay at the Hound Hotel is like a holiday for your dog. We have a large play park, plenty of toys and a pool for the dogs to play in, in the summer. Your dog will love playing with the other guests.

HOUND HOTEL
WHO'S WHO

WINIFRED WOLFE

Hound Hotel is run by Winifred Wolfe, a lifelong dog lover. Winifred loves all types of dogs. She likes to get to know every breed. When she's not taking care of the canines, she writes books about — that's right — dogs.

ALFIE AND ALFREEDA WOLFE

Winifred's twins help out as much as they can. Whether your dog needs gentle attention or extra playtime, Alfreeda and Alfie provide special services you can't find anywhere else. Your dog will never get bored whilst these two are helping out.

WOLFGANG WOLFE

Winifred's husband helps out at the hotel whenever he can, but he spends most of his time travelling to study packs of wolves. Wolfgang is a real wolf lover — he even named his children after pack leaders, the alpha wolves. Every wolf pack has two alpha wolves: a male wolf and a female wolf, just like the Wolfe family twins.

Next time your family goes on holiday, bring your dog to Hound Hotel.

Your pooch is sure to have a howling good time!

CHAPTER 1
Howling like mad

I'm Alfie Wolfe, and I'm here to tell you all about a scaredy-cat dog called Freddie.

I'm not making fun of him. I know what it's like to be scared of things. Especially sharks. Gosh, sharks are scary!

But this story isn't about killer fish. It's about Freddie. Freddie the beagle. Freddie with a howl like you wouldn't believe.

He stayed at our dog hotel last June. I'll never forget that stormy week. There were huge, dark thunder clouds. Those clouds were the colour of a stormy sea full of seaweed. And sharks.

Back to Freddie. He arrived on a Saturday. The weather lady on TV had forecast blue sky and sunshine on that weekend. She certainly got that wrong!

That morning, a huge crash of thunder woke me up. I was lying inside my sleeping bag on our living room floor. I was at the end of a nightmare – still half asleep – and shouting out, "Help! I'm inside a shark! It swallowed me whole!"

I kicked and punched and pulled, trying to burst my way out of that shark's stomach. A loud ripping sound, a bit like meat being torn off bones, made me stop and open my eyes.

I realized that I was at the bottom of my sleeping bag. All of me. My whole head and

bibliotheca SelfCheck System

libraries ni
www.librariesni.org.uk

Cookstown Library
13 Burn Road
Cookstown
BT80 8DJ

Customer ID: ******7044

Items that you have borrowed

Title: Fearless Freddie
ID: C901603782
Due: 09 December 2021

Total items: 1
Account balance: £0.00
18/11/2021 15:27
Borrowed: 1
Overdue: 0
Hold requests: 1
Ready for collection: 0

t: 028 8676 3702
e: cookstown.library@librariesni.org.uk

body! Then I noticed that I'd torn a big hole in the bag.

I stuck my head out of the tear and looked around.

Our living room was as dark as the inside of a shark's stomach. It was noisy, too. I heard my own panting and rain pounding on the windows. I heard thunder rumbling outside and my sister laughing.

I looked over at Alfreeda and saw that she was inside her sleeping bag. But she was down at the very bottom of it, all curled up, laughing at me.

Her sleeping bag looked like a shark that had swallowed up a whole child.

"Ha!" she cried. "You're afraid of sharks now *too*? When did that happen? We don't live anywhere near the sea! Ha-ha-ha!"

Suddenly an enormous bolt of thunder silenced her.

I thought, *That's strange. Alfreeda is never quiet. And since when* HAVE *I been afraid of sharks?* Then I remembered – they had only started frightening me the night before.

My family had been watching another film about dogs. Well, my dad hadn't been watching. He was in Canada, studying wolves in the wilderness. Just my mum, sister and I watched it, snug in our sleeping bags on the floor.

Somewhere in the middle of the film, Mum had moved to the sofa and fallen asleep. The second the film ended, Alfreeda started to snore like a pig.

I got up to turn off the TV but sat right back down. A shark film had come on, and I was interested. It was about a killer great white shark. The huge shark had terrified everyone in a town by the sea.

Before I even realized it, I'd watched the whole thing.

After that, it took me forever to fall asleep. I just kept chewing my fingernails, like a dog with a tasty bone. Or like a shark chewing on someone's tasty leg.

I must've finally nodded off, though, because there I was, waking up the next morning. Super-bright flashes of lightning turned the whole living room white – as white as a great white shark's underside.

Loud claps of thunder made our windows shake. My sister was still curled up at the bottom of her sleeping bag. The bumpy lump of knees and elbows shook all over.

I couldn't believe she was laughing that hard at me, so hard that no noise came out. When somebody laughs that hard, the only thing that comes out is tears from their eyeballs.

It's not as though I could laugh at her and call her a scaredy-cat. You see, my sister is fearless. I hate it! She's not even scared of Spot, our cockerel.

It's not as though I'm scared of *all* cockerels. But Spot charges at us like a bull when he's bored. It's really strange. Alfreeda always laughs. I scream.

It's not fair that she's Alpha Kid in the Bravery Department in this house. It must be because she was born five minutes before me. It's so unfair.

Suddenly I heard Mum say, "Good morning, sleepyheads. Are you two awake?" Her voice crackled over the walkie-talkie.

Alfreeda leapt out of her sleeping bag. She tore across the room and grabbed the walkie-talkie off of the charger.

She pressed the *Talk* button and shouted, "Mum! Mum! Hi! Hi! Over! Over!"

"Why on earth are you shouting, Alfreeda?" Mum asked in that crackling voice. "And why are you repeating yourself? Never mind. I need you two down at the kennels on the double. The thunder is scaring Freddie, the little beagle," Mum's voice crackled on. "He's howling like mad and making the other dogs bark. I need one of you to calm him down, the other to do some jobs for me. Please hurry! Don't forget to brush your teeth. Over."

"We'll be right there, Mum!" Alfreeda shouted. "I'll look after Freddie. I'll calm him down. Alfie will do *all* of the jobs. Over! Over!"

"No way!" I shouted. "*I* want Freddie! Give me the walkie. Let me talk to Mum!"

Alfreeda laughed and raced up the stairs holding the walkie-talkie.

CHAPTER 2

A scream that can break glass

I tried to jump up and run after my sister. But I got tangled up in my sleeping bag. Finally I ripped my way out and sprinted up the stairs after her.

Alfreeda was in her silly bedroom. I stepped in and shook my head at all her stuffed-toy dogs. There must have been at least a hundred. Maybe two.

"Good luck finding the walkie-talkie," she said and grinned. "It's behind one of my dogs. Have fun doing boring jobs while I play with Freddie."

"Wrong!" I shouted.

"Let's see," she said and grinned. Then she dashed to the bathroom.

"You're *not* going to get to Freddie first!" I screamed. I dashed to my room to get dressed.

I dug through some piles of clothes on my floor. I looked everywhere for my jeans.

Then I saw them. They were on my legs. Just like that, I remembered – I'd slept in my jeans and a Hound Hotel T-shirt.

Ha! I was way ahead of my sister! I was ready to have some fun with my new friend Freddie. Then I remembered – Mum had reminded me to brush my teeth.

I raced into the bathroom.

My sister was already at the sink, brushing her teeth. She was dressed for kennel work, too. Everyday it's the same – blue jeans and a Hound Hotel T-shirt.

Then I remembered that she'd slept in her clothes, too. I groaned.

She spun around. "Why don't you knock?" she screamed. Her mouth was full of foamy toothpaste.

"The door was open!" I screamed back. "Stop screaming! You're spraying me with toothpaste!"

I wiped my cheeks and chin. Disgusting!

She spun back around and brushed faster.

Lightning-quick, I grabbed my toothbrush and squeezed on some toothpaste. The whole glob fell off the brush. It landed on the floor with a *splat*.

"You're cleaning that up," she said in her I'm-the-boss voice.

I frowned at her. My heart began to pound.
Toothpaste covered her mouth. And her eyes
had her normal morning look – dead-looking
and beady-like. Like a certain kind of killer fish.

She spat the foam into the sink and grabbed
a glass to rinse out her mouth. She rinsed
and spat, then had a quick drink of water. She
swallowed her drink and turned to me. Her
beady eyes stared right into mine.

"What are you *staring* at?" she demanded. She spoke right into the empty glass.

Well, the bottom of the glass magnified her teeth. I'm telling you, they looked *huge*! And extra pointy! And extremely *sharp*!

I screamed – the kind of scream that's so loud it could break glass. That same second, three other things happened: thunder crashed and shook the house; Alfreeda screamed her head off; Alfreeda dropped her glass.

It shattered across the bathroom floor. It broke into hundreds of tiny pieces.

"You're cleaning that up," I said.

"No I'm not," she said.

"Yes you are," I said. "You dropped it."

"Well, you screamed and *made* me drop it," she said.

"You screamed too," I said.

"I screamed because *you* screamed," she said. "Why *else* would I scream?"

She had a point.

Alfreeda put her toothbrush away in our dog-shaped toothbrush holder. "See you outside," she said. "Have fun doing all of your jobs." She leapt over the broken glass and landed in the doorway.

"No!" I shouted. "*I'm* playing with Freddie!"

— CHAPTER 3 —
Call me a scaredy-cat

Alfreeda turned around. She leaned on the doorframe and sighed.

"Oh, Alfie," she said in her tired-teacher voice. "*Please* listen. Freddie doesn't want to *play* now. He's *scared*. He needs me to hug him. And cuddle him. He needs me to say, 'It's okay,' over and over. Understand?"

She had a point. Five points, to be exact.

"Anyway," she said and rolled her eyes, "how could *you* make a scared dog feel better?"

Go on then, I thought. *Call me a scaredy-cat to my face. I dare you.*

"Don't hurt yourself doing all this cleaning," she said. "So long!" She ran down the stairs. The back door slammed.

One second later, I heard a fierce clap of thunder and a shriek so loud it could've broken glass (if the glass hadn't already been broken).

The shriek came from outside. "Must have been an owl," I said to myself as I grabbed the broom.

Even though *I* didn't break it, I swept up the glass as quickly as I could. I only got one little cut on my small finger.

That made me think about the cut a shark could make on someone's fingers. It would be more like, goodbye *whole* hand!

Just thinking about it made me shake all

over. I went back to brushing my teeth, but I kept missing the toothbrush with the paste. A few more globs fell on the floor.

Finally, I covered the brush in toothpaste. Then, faster than a shark can bite, I brushed my teeth. It only took about two seconds flat.

Don't think I'm bragging about my alpha-boy speed in toothbrushing. The trick is in the toothbrush. You see, Mum buys a special kind for my sister and me. They're extra big so they clean more teeth in less time!

The fact is, they're dog toothbrushes. That's the only aisle in the supermarket that Mum likes to shop in – the pet aisle. The brushes may be shaped like dog chews, but they work really well. I threw my brush into the holder, spat out my toothpaste and ran downstairs.

Somehow, *I'd* get to play with good old Freddie *and* get out of doing the stupid jobs.

I dashed down our driveway to the kennel building. I got completely soaked in about two seconds flat. If I remember correctly, I think I dodged a few bolts of lightning too.

It was actually quite good fun. But not as much fun as I was going to have with Freddie! I threw open the front door of our dog hotel.

"Hello, Freddie!" I announced. "Get ready to party! Here comes Alfie!"

I don't think he heard me. An awful lot of

howling and barking was coming from the kennels.

I dashed through the office, down the hall and into the big room at the back of the building. That's where the pens are. Or you can call them kennels. You can even call them runs if you like.

You see, each run is big enough for a dog to run around inside. Get it?

I spotted Freddie straight away, at least ... I spotted his nose! He was under his raised bed. (That's like a toddler's bed, raised off of the ground on short legs.) Freddie was hiding under his. He'd stopped howling now. The other dogs had gone quiet, too.

Still, he was shivering uncontrollably and making quiet little crying sounds. Alfreeda was on her knees, wiggling her fingers at him.

"Come on out now, little one," she said in her talking-to-babies voice. "That horrible thunder is all over. You're okay, you're okay…"

He kept shivering.

"Oh, yes, you're really calming him down, aren't you?" I said to my sister.

She spun around and shouted, "Stop creeping up on me like that!"

"I didn't creep up on you!" I said.

"Yes you did!" she said and stared hard at me. Gosh! Her eyes are so beady.

I froze, locked in a staring battle, like a clown fish facing a great white shark. Finally, I tore my eyeballs away and pretended to read some information about Freddie.

Freddie's check-in form was on a clipboard that hung on the front of his kennel door. I soon got bored just standing there, so I actually started to read it. This is what Freddie's owner had written:

Dear Hound Hotel workers,

Please beware when taking Freddie on walks … he's fearless. He'll chase a horse. He'll charge a bull. Freddie is only afraid of one thing – thunder. However, the weather forecast promises sunshine for the whole weekend. So all should be well.

I'm sure Freddie will have nothing but fun at your lovely hotel. Thank you.

Best wishes,

Bob (Freddie's owner)

"What fun?" I said to myself. Freddie hadn't had a speck of fun yet!

Well, you can't be lazy when you run a dog hotel. I had to get cracking and help give good old Fred the best holiday he'd ever had!

I marched into his kennel. He was still under his bed. Alfreeda was still begging him to come out, in that strange talking-to-babies voice.

"I'll handle this," I said. "Move over."

"No," she said.

"Mum!" I shouted.

CHAPTER 4

Definitely not funny

Mum came walking in from the utility room. She was carrying a big basket of clean dog towels and blankets. She put the basket on a little table with wheels and wheeled the table into the middle of the room.

As she started to fold the laundry, she smiled at me. "Good morning, Alfie," she said.

"It's *not* a good morning," I said. "Alfreeda's hogging Freddie."

"Oh, you two silly dog lovers," Mum said.

"Always fighting over who gets to play with the cutest dogs. I don't blame you! But guess what, Alfie? I have some great-fun jobs for you. A little Chihuahua has just checked in. Would you please go to the storeroom and gather some overnight things for him? Grab an extra-small bed, a little blanket, a tiny water bowl —"

"I can't see a Chihuahua," I said, looking around.

"He's in his outside run," Mum said. "In kennel number four."

I looked at the doggie door at the back of that kennel. You see, every guest at our hotel has an outdoor run, too.

"What's his name?" I asked.

"Shark," Mum said.

I spun around and said, "That's *definitely* not funny, Mum."

"What's not funny?" she asked.

"Joking about his name," I said.

"Why would I joke about something like that?" Mum said, handing me a towel. "Please dry him off when he comes inside. Oh look, there's Shark now."

Nice and slowly, I turned around. I stared through the wire-mesh fence at the little teeny-tiny dog. He stood as stiff as a shark fin, right in front of the doggie door he'd just pushed through. He dripped water all over the floor, as though he'd just jumped out of the sea.

"Go on, Alfie," Mum said. "Go into his kennel and dry him off. Quickly, before he gets cold."

I held the towel tightly against my chest. I stepped towards Shark's pen. I stared at him. He stared at me. He took a step in my direction. He narrowed his eyes at me and growled.

Then he opened his mouth extremely wide! I saw masses of pointy, sharp-looking teeth. *Shark teeth!*

Just then, four things happened at exactly the same time: Shark sprang straight towards me; I screamed; a super-loud crash of thunder shook the building; Alfreeda gave a terrible shriek.

I jumped back and knocked over the little table on wheels. Clean blankets and towels flew *everywhere!*

"Alfie!" Mum cried. "I've just folded those!"

❧ CHAPTER 5 ❧
Stop it!

Wow! Freddie really howled at that last crash of thunder. He closed his eyes and threw back his head with a "*Wah-oooohhh!*"

His howl made all five of the big dogs bark. Shark started too. I could see every big tooth inside that little dog's mouth.

At some point, Freddie leapt onto Alfreeda's lap. That's where he was now, shaking and shivering. He shook so hard that he made my sister shake too.

Mum didn't say anything to anyone. She just calmly picked up the table. Then she picked up all the towels and blankets. Next, she walked into Shark's pen. She picked him up, dried him off with a towel and kissed him on the head.

After she had settled Shark in his kennel, she put on music. She turned the volume up high.

Ugh. The first song she played was my sister's favourite. The song was the most annoying pop song of all time. Part of it goes like this: "Oh baby, I'm lovin' our happy, sunshine-y, baby-blue-sky day."

I hate that song. Almost more than sharks. But Freddie stopped howling straight away. The other dogs stopped barking too. Maybe the song had brainwashed the dogs.

Alfreeda buried her face into the back of Freddie's neck. She rocked him backwards and forwards and kept saying, "It's okay, it's okay."

Freddie started to shiver again.

Before the song even ended, Mum turned down the volume. *Thank. You. Mum.*

She started to fold the laundry again. "So, Alfie and Alfreeda," she said and smiled at us. "A minute ago, you were both screaming as though the world was about to end. Do you want to talk about it?"

"No," Alfreeda and I said at the same time.

"Okay," said Mum with a smile.

That second, more thunder rumbled. Lightning flashed. My sister buried her face into Freddie's neck again. Poor thing. What if her nose was running or something? Disgusting!

Poor Freddie was having no fun at all. I had to unscare him so we could play catch or something. Maybe I'd build him a storm-chaser van, and we'd pretend to zoom after tornadoes and stuff like that.

But I had to calm him down first! And I knew exactly how to do it.

"Hey, Freddie, old boy," I said. "I'll put on the tumble dryer for you. The humming will calm you down, really quickly. You see, once a stray cat jumped out of a tree and landed on our dad's back. Dad sat by the dryer for about an hour before he calmed down."

Alfreeda looked at me and smiled a little.

"Oh, yeah," she said. "I remember that. Dad's so scared of cats. Let's go, Freddie."

She picked him up and carried him to the utility room. I followed.

"Wait, Alfie," Mum called. "What about your jobs?"

"But Freddie needs me," I called over my shoulder. "I'm the Alfie Male in this pack. It's my job to get the underdogs unscared!"

"All right," she said and laughed.

I dashed to the utility room. Alfreeda had already started the tumble dryer. It rattled and thumped.

She sat on the floor and leaned against the dryer. Freddie was in her lap. She kept saying, "It's okay."

But the thunder was getting even louder.

The rain was coming down harder, too. It hammered the window above the dryer.

I climbed on top of the dryer and looked outside. "Oh no!" I said. "The park's flooded! It's never rained this much before."

"I know," Alfreeda said. Her voice came out a bit squeaky.

"You're speaking really strangely," I said.

"No I'm not," she squeaked.

I shrugged and said, "Do you know what? If the park is flooded, that means the lake is too." The lake was on the other side of the hill, not far from the park.

"And that means the rivers are flooded," I said. My voice was coming out squeaky now, too. "If the rivers are flooded, the sea will be too. That means that sharks could be swimming upriver from the sea."

"They could be swimming from the river to the lake to the park," I squeaked on. "They're waiting out there for us, with their jaws wide open! When the sun comes out, we'll go outside to play, and sharks will turn us into their afternoon snack!"

My heart pounded like a hammerhead shark. I looked at my sister. Her eyes rolled so far back in her head that they turned almost completely white.

"Stop it!" I cried.

She unrolled her eyeballs and sighed. "Alfie," she said in her tired-teacher voice. "You're not making sense. We live miles and miles away from the sea. Sharks can't swim this far. Anyway, they need salt water. Plus, sharks don't even like to eat humans. We're too bony."

"Really?" I squeaked.

"Yes," she said. "A shark takes a bite out of someone's leg, says yuck, and spits it out."

"Then why do they bite people in the first place?" I demanded.

"Because they think we're nice fat juicy seals," she said.

"Me?" I cried.

"Not you!" she said. "There aren't any sharks around here, Alfie! What's *wrong* with you?"

"Uh, I watched a shark film last night," I said. I told her the name of the film.

"Are you joking?" she said, her eyes wide. "Wow. Does Mum know?"

I shook my head.

"That's supposed to be the scariest film of all time," Alfreeda said. "Well, trust me, Alf. There are *no* sharks near us, okay?"

I was trying my best to believe her when an enormous clap of thunder went *BOOM*! Freddie bolted off Alfreeda's lap. He started to howl and raced out of the utility room.

Alfreeda jumped up and chased after him. "Freddie, come back, it's okay," she called. Her voice came out all whispery. And I know why, too...

Because she'd just screamed her head off! It's true! I'd seen it with my own eyeballs. I'd heard it with my own eardrums. She'd opened her big mouth even wider and screamed so loudly that she'd lost her voice!

I couldn't believe it. My sister, Alpha Girl, was *scared of thunder*. She never used to be but – for some reason – she was now! *Ha!*

I leapt off of the tumble dryer and chased after her. I couldn't wait to laugh in her face.

— CHAPTER 6 —
Sir Lightning Bolt

It turned out that I couldn't laugh in my sister's face. I couldn't even see her face.

I found Alfreeda and Freddie in the storeroom. A blanket covered Alfreeda's head and whole body. Freddie was under the blanket with her. He was howling his head off.

I pulled the blanket off them. Freddie looked at me and stopped howling straight away.

"Hey!" I said in a really firm voice. "Why are you acting as though you're scared of thunder and lightning?"

"Don't shout at Freddie," she said. "He can't help it."

"Not him!" I said. "I'm talking to you! Look, *you* can't be scared of thunder and lightning – or anything! Someone's got to be the bravest in the pack around here. Remember the time a stray cat jumped onto Mum's head in the chicken coop? She screamed her head off." Both of our parents are afraid of cats!

"You're the only completely brave top dog around here!" I added in my firmest voice. "You *have* to be strong – so that the underdogs around here will feel safer!"

"I c-c-can't," she whispered.

"What happened?" I asked. "You never used to be scared of thunderstorms."

"I'll tell you what happened," she said. "Yesterday Mum and I took some dogs on a walk through the woods. We saw this really big tree, split in half, with burn marks on it. Lightning had hit it! But listen to this: lots of smaller pieces of wood had split off the tree and sprayed all over the place. They must've been flying really fast because they were stuck in other trees, just like arrows! If animals or people had been nearby ... it would've been awful." Alfreeda stopped talking and shivered.

"Wow," I said. "Amazing! I'd love to see that! Anyway, you're safe in here. There aren't any windows. Lightning can't get in."

"I'm still totally terrified. I can still hear the thunder," she squeaked. "And maybe there's a crack in the wall. Lightning could get in and strike my toes or something."

"Lightning can strike through cracks?" I asked.

She nodded, sure of herself.

My sister was the best fact collector in our house, too. So I just shrugged and said, "Oh."

Then I had an idea. "I know," I said. "We could build a lightning-safe wall. Thick and solid, like a castle. Let's do it!"

"No," Alfreeda said. She pulled the blanket over her head and Freddie's head, too.

"Fine," I said. "I'll build it myself."

"Hurry," said Alfreeda. "Freddie's got bad breath. I can't stay under here for much longer."

"No problem," I said. Then, at alpha-boy speed, I built a tall castle wall, right in front of the two scaredy-cats.

First, I found a pile of big boxes. They were full of dog treats and toys and stuff. Nothing too heavy.

Next, I positioned a row of five boxes in a

line. Then I stacked four more rows on top of that one. I stood on a chair to build the top row.

"The rampart's done," I said.

"The what?" asked Alfreeda.

"The rampart – the wall," I said. "Now I'll build the battlement."

"The what?" she asked.

"You'll see," I said, grabbing some small boxes. I put them in a row on top of the rampart, but I left a large space between each one.

"I've finished the battlement," I said. "See? You can look between the boxes. You can see straight away if anyone bad is coming. If you see Sir Lightning Bolt blasting straight at you, get your bow and arrow ready.

"If you see his ghost-white knights and his ghost-white war horses coming, too, make sure

you have some bows and arrows at the ready," I added. "Make sure Freddie has a bow and arrow too."

"I can't see over the top," she said. "Even when I'm standing on tiptoes. The wall's too high."

"Oh," I said. "Well, don't you feel safer? How about Freddie? Is he feeling better? I've completely boxed you in."

"A box has four sides," she said.

"Okay, I've *triangled* you in," I said. "Same thing."

"Why are there tiny cracks between all the big boxes?" she asked.

"They're arrow slits," I said.

"Alfie," she said in that same old tired-teacher voice. "Freddie and I don't have arrows. Or bows. And anyway, lightning would burn them down. And there's no drawbridge. How are we supposed to get out of here?"

"I'll be right back," I said and ran to the office.

I dug in the desk drawer and found a felt-tip

pen. I dashed back into the storeroom and drew some lines on the big boxes, super speedily.

"There," I said. "I drawed a bridge."

"You *drew* a bridge," Alfreeda corrected me.

"I drew a drawbridge," I said. "Same thing."

She started to shout, "A drawn drawbridge isn't any good! Get us *out* of here!"

She must've started to kick the boxes because they all tumbled down, right on top of my head. I shoved the boxes off, then rubbed my head and arms and shoulders. Nothing hurt too badly.

I stared at my strange sister. Her hands were on her hips. She frowned at me.

"What?" I asked.

Just then, loud thunder rumbled outside. Alfreeda started to shiver all over again.

"Look," she said in a shaky voice, "I gave *you* the shark facts. You need to give me the *lightning* facts! Tell me there aren't any cracks in these walls! Tell me that lightning can't come through cracks anyway! Tell me that, yes, lightning can maybe come through an open window, but we don't have any windows open!

She kept on squeaking. "And tell me that thunder's nothing to be scared of, because when you hear it, lightning has already struck somewhere else! Tell me that thunder can't hurt you! You need to be *firm* about the facts, Alfie!"

"You just were," I said.

"But I don't believe me," she squeaked. "Maybe I'd believe *you*."

"That doesn't make any sense," I said. "Just snap out of it. What about Freddie, eh? He hasn't had any fun with you in charge. Come on, Freddie. Let's go and play."

I clapped and whistled. "Let's go, Freddie," I said. "Let's play catch in the office." I grabbed a ball off a shelf.

He didn't move. Then I realized that he couldn't. He was wrapped very tightly in that blanket.

"What have you done?" I asked my sister. "How many times have you wrapped this blanket around Freddie?"

"Seven," she said.

"Well, unwrap him," I said. "He's not a hotdog."

"No," she said. "It makes him feel safer."

"No it doesn't," I said. "Look, he's still shivering."

Even louder thunder rumbled outside. "Alfie?" my sister squeaked. "Would you please go and get my sleeping bag?"

"Why should I?" I asked.

"If I feel safer, then I can make Freddie feel safer," she said. "I'll give you fifty pence."

"A pound," I said.

"It's a deal," she agreed.

I kicked boxes out of the way and headed towards the door.

"Alf?" she squeaked.

"What?" I said over my shoulder.

"You're going outside, in the middle of this terrible thunderstorm, for *me?*" she squeaked.

"No!" I said. "For Freddie!"

"Well," Alfreeda said, "when it comes to bravery, you're the Al—"

"There's no time to talk," I interrupted her. "I'll get my sleeping bag, too. And some pillows, and leftover popcorn from last night. We'll have a sleepover in Freddie's kennel. Then he won't have to sleep all on his scaredy-cat own tonight. *Finally* some fun. I'll be back in a minute."

I raced outside, into the pouring rain, and leapt over every puddle. Just in case some baby sharks had swum upriver by mistake.

CHAPTER 7

I'm a goner!

Before we knew it, we were all back in Freddie's kennel together.

Alfreeda and Freddie were inside her sleeping bag. She looked like shark lunch, all curled up at the bottom.

Freddie sat in the middle. Every time he howled at loud thunder, he threw back his head. The howling lump in Freddie's throat looked just like a shark's fin.

"This is boring," I said.

Nobody heard me. Mum was playing some really loud pop music and singing along. She was grooming a big poodle too. She kept dancing around the poodle, brushing to the beat of the music.

The big dogs watched her. The thunder wasn't making them shiver or anything. No. Mum and the big dogs were acting like it was a sunshine-y, baby-blue-sky day.

I looked at Shark. He was sitting in the kennel next door and staring at Alfreeda's shivering mass. He shivered, too.

"Oi, Shark," I said. "Stop staring at my sister."

He looked at me.

"Do you know," I said to him, "you can catch a bad case of fear, just like a bad cold. If you hang around with a scaredy-cat for too long, you can catch it. Even if you're a dog. Look at the big dogs who are watching my mum. They're as calm as anything."

Shark looked back at Alfreeda. He started to shiver again. I got up and marched into his kennel. I picked him up, marched out and headed towards the office.

About halfway there, I realized that Shark's teeth were about ten centimetres from my neck. My heart started to pound. *I'm a goner!* I thought. *I'm shark meat! Goodbye sweet life!*

But I stopped and said to myself in a firm voice, "I'm fine." And guess what, I was!

I headed towards the office desk and pulled open the top drawer. Placing Shark inside, I said, "Dig away, little man. I'm looking for a deck of cards. I know it's in here somewhere. Can you help me find it?"

Well, that tiny Chihuahua started to dig like

a terrier. But he was no help at all in finding those fifty-two cards.

He kept bumping his nose against Mum's silly old mask. It had a fake nose, fake glasses and a fake moustache. When my sister and I were little, we were sometimes a bit scared of the big dogs. Mum put on the mask to make us laugh. When mum was wearing the mask, we completely forgot to be scared.

Shark bumped the mask again with his nose. "Do you want to try it on?" I asked.

He yapped, which I decided meant yes. I put the mask on him. It was far too big for his tiny head.

"Wear it as long as you like," I said. "We could do with having a laugh around here today."

Then I did a bit more digging and found the deck of cards.

"Okay, Shark," I said, "here's the plan. First, we'll unscare my sister. Then Freddie. It has to be in that order because Freddie thinks Alfreeda is his pack leader. Understand?"

Shark looked at me through the ridiculous mask.

I laughed, and we walked back to Freddie's kennel.

❧— CHAPTER 8 —❧
Hurray! I won again

A few seconds later, I poked Alfreeda's knee. Or maybe it was her elbow.

"Hello," I said. "Do you want to play War?"

"No," she said.

I couldn't believe my ears! War was my sister's absolute favourite card game. I hated it because she always won. How she could win a game of chance every time, I do not know.

"You can shuffle," I said.

"Do you want to flip a coin for it?" she asked.

"No," I said. "I'm letting you shuffle first. Come on."

"Okay," she said and squeezed past Freddie. She crawled out and grabbed the cards from me.

Then she saw Shark and laughed. The laugh was weak, but it was definitely a laugh.

We sat on top of my torn-up sleeping bag. Alfreeda started to shuffle.

"You can watch," I said to Shark. He sat between us.

Suddenly a big crash of thunder made Alfreeda jump into the air. She screamed and threw all the cards across the room.

I didn't even lose my cool. "Look," I said. "It's raining cards. Don't worry. I'll pick them up."

Alfreeda looked sideways at me. "You're acting very strangely, Alfie Wolfe," she said.

For once in my life I didn't say, "You're even more strange, Alfreeda Wolfe." I just crawled around Freddie's kennel, at lightning speed and picked up all the cards.

That put Alfreeda in a good mood. Beating me at War three times in a row put her in an event better mood. She kept shouting, "I declare war!" and winning every time.

After the second game, I hauled Freddie out of Alfreeda's sleeping bag. I held him on my lap. He kept looking backwards and forwards between Shark and my sister.

We started a fourth game. She shouted, "I declare war!" for about the hundredth time.

With no warning, a huge crash of thunder rattled the windows.

Alfreeda collected her cards and cried, "Hurray! I won again."

I tapped her arm. "Guess what?" I said.

"What?" she asked.

"It just thundered really loudly," I said.

"No it didn't," she said.

"Yes it did," I said. "You didn't jump or scream."

"Really?" she asked. "Wow. And look, Freddie's not howling!"

"That's because he's watching you," I said. "I've worked it out."

"Worked what out?" she asked.

"Dogs look to their leader, don't they." I said. "Well, dogs don't understand what thunder is. They look to their leader to work out how to behave. If you act like nothing's wrong, he'll feel brave too."

Alfreeda stared at me for about a minute. Then she said, "Do you know what, Alf? That actually makes sense."

"Of course it does," I said. "Now, do you want to play storm chasers with the dogs? We could use that little table on wheels and build a storm-chaser van. Freddie and Shark could sit inside it. We could pretend to chase all kinds of extreme weather! We could make storm documentaries!"

"Yes!" she said. "We could build a dashboard, with a computer on it."

"And a satellite dish for the top of the van," I said.

"Fab," she said. "I'll go and get some felt-tip pens and an empty box."

"Grab the table, too," I said. "We'll play catch in the office until you get there. Come on, Fred and Shark Man. I'll race you!"

The three of us raced to the office. Freddie won.

I pushed all the furniture out of the way, then threw the ball to Freddie. He caught it in his mouth, first time!

Then Shark and I chased him around, trying to get the ball back. We couldn't catch him.

Well, Freddie was just doing what beagles do best – racing around and around and never getting tired!

"We're finally having some fun!" I said.

Freddie grinned at me and dropped the ball. I'm. Not. Kidding.

Good old Fred *grinned*.

Is a beagle the dog for you?

Hi! It's me, Alfreeda!

I'm sure you'd love to have your own cute, adorable beagle now too, wouldn't you? Of course you would! Beagles LOVE kids and make great pets for families! But before you dash off to buy or adopt one, here are some important facts you should know:

Beagles are really active! They'll play for hours ... then want to keep on playing! They love to run around outside and play all kinds of games. So if you're the kind of family that likes to stay inside and watch TV a lot, DON'T get a beagle (or any dog). Get a pet rock.

Beagles LOVE to eat, and they eat a LOT. Some can eat more than bigger dogs. On walks, they'll try to eat anything they find laying on the ground. Beagles have a very strong sense of smell and can find food that's hidden away, too. They could become overweight quickly if they don't get enough exercise. If you can't promise to play with your beagle and walk with her every day, do NOT get one. Paint your pet rock to look like a beagle.

Beagles follow their powerful smelling noses everywhere! They'll race down the road or into the park, chasing one curious smell after another. It's easy for a beagle to get lost. They HAVE to be on leads or in a fenced-in garden to stay safe outside.

Okay, signing off for now ... until the next adventure at Hound Hotel!

Yours very factually,

Alfreeda Wolfe

Glossary

battlement   low wall at the top of a tower or other wall, with openings along it for soldiers to shoot through

brainwash   make someone accept and believe something by saying it over and over again

demand   ask for something firmly

disgusting   very unpleasant and offensive to others

forecast   prediction that something might happen in the future

howling   loud, sad noise

lightning   flash of light in the sky when electricity moves between clouds or between a cloud and the ground

magnify   make something appear larger

rampart   surrounding wall or embankment of a fort or castle built to protect against attack

shatter   break into tiny pieces

shriek   loud, piercing cry

wilderness   area of wild land where no people live, such as a dense forest

Talk about it

1. Parents often don't let their children watch scary films, like the shark film in this book. Why do you think parents make this rule?

2. Why was it important that Freddie didn't see others being afraid?

3. On page 68, Alfreeda has shared some facts (and opinions) about beagles. Do you think a beagle would be a good dog for your family? Why or why not?

Write about it

1. In this book, the characters dealt with their fears in various ways, including talking about it or distracting themselves with other things. Write a paragraph describing how you deal with your fears.

2. Write a letter to the twin's dad about Freddie. Use either Alfie's or Alfreeda's point of view.

3. Put together a factsheet about beagles. Use three or more reputable sources to help you.

About the author

Shelley Swanson Sateren grew up with five pet dogs –
a beagle, a terrier mix, a terrier-poodle mix, a
Weimaraner and a German shorthaired pointer. As an
adult, she adopted a lively West Highland white terrier
called Max. Apart from writing many children's books,
Shelley has worked as a children's book editor and in a
children's bookshop. She lives in Minnesota, USA, with
her husband, and has two grown-up sons.

About the illustrator

Deborah Melmon has worked as an illustrator for
over 25 years. After graduating from the Academy of
Art University in San Francisco, she began her career
illustrating covers for a weekly magazine supplement.
Since then, she has produced artwork for over twenty
children's books. Her artwork can also be found on
wrapping paper, greeting cards and fabric. Deborah
lives in California, USA, and shares her studio with an
energetic Airedale terrier called Mack.

ADVENTURES AT HOUND HOTEL
Fearless Freddie

WRITTEN BY Shelley Swanson Sateren
ILLUSTRATED BY Deborah Melmon

ADVENTURES AT HOUND HOTEL
Growling Gracie

WRITTEN BY Shelley Swanson Sateren
ILLUSTRATION BY Deborah Melmon

ADVENTURES AT HOUND HOTEL
Homesick Herbie

WRITTEN BY Shelley Swanson Sateren
ILLUSTRATION BY Deborah Melmon

ADVENTURES AT HOUND HOTEL
Mudball Molly

WRITTEN BY Shelley Swanson Sateren
ILLUSTRATED BY Deborah Melmon